NO LONGER PROPERTY OF
SEATTLE PUBLIC LIBRARY

For Kaztah

with love

and for Delia x

Copyright © 2007 by Sue Heap

All rights reserved. No part of this book may be reproduced, transmitted, or stored in an information retrieval system in any form or by any means, graphic, electronic, or mechanical, including photocopying, taping, and recording, without prior written permission from the publisher.

First U.S. edition 2008

Library of Congress Cataloging-in-Publication Data is available.

Library of Congress Catalog Card Number pending.

ISBN 978-0-7636-3654-8

10 9 8 7 6 5 4 3 2 1

Printed in China

This book was typeset in Franklin Gothic. The illustrations were done in pencil and acrylic.

Candlewick Press
2067 Massachusetts Avenue
Cambridge, Massachusetts 02140

visit us at www.candlewick.com

and Daniel

and Dan & Deirdre

CANDLEWICK PRESS
CAMBRIDGE, MASSACHUSETTS

and my Dad.

Danny's Drawing Book

Sue Heap

ZC

I'm Danny. This is me
with my yellow drawing book.
Next to me is my friend Ettie.
And this is how we made a story
when we went to the zoo
on a snowy day.

ENTRANCE

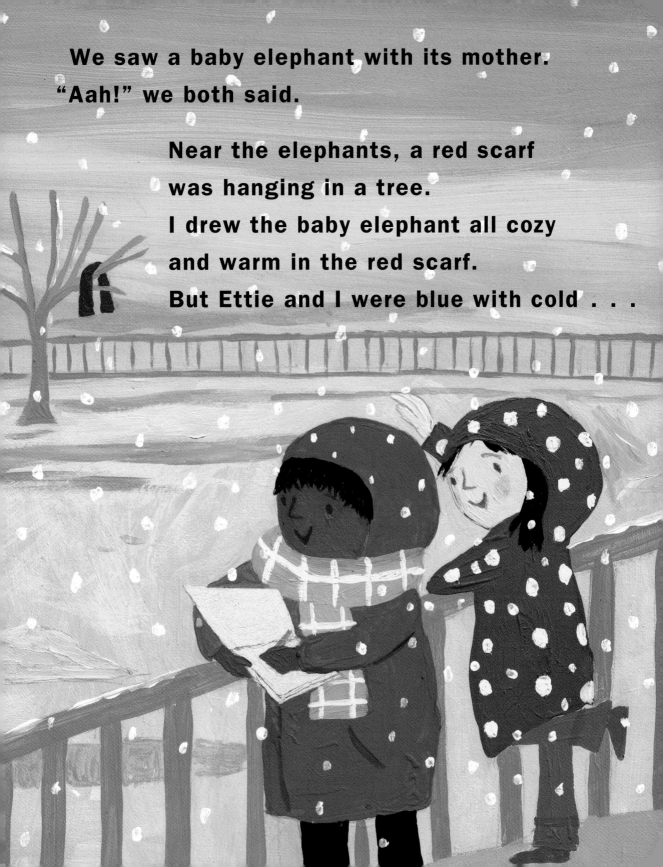

We saw a baby elephant with its mother.
"Aah!" we both said.

Near the elephants, a red scarf
was hanging in a tree.
I drew the baby elephant all cozy
and warm in the red scarf.
But Ettie and I were blue with cold . . .

so we went into the Nocturnal Animal House. That's where the animals who stay awake at night live. As our eyes slowly got used to the dark, we saw a very unusual animal.

Ettie read the sign. "He's an aardvark, and he comes from Africa. He lives underground in a burrow." "Hello, aardvark!" we whispered.

I drew the
aardvark next
to the elephant.

"I think they
like each
other,"
said Ettie.

She was right. They did!

I decided that the aardvark needed a hat, so I drew him a green one. Then I added a suitcase and some cookies.

The aardvark wanted to go to Africa.
The elephant wanted to go, too.

But they didn't know how to get there.

The elephant had lots of ideas.

But the aardvark didn't like any of them.

I told them I could help and that Ettie and I wanted to come, too. So I drew us in my drawing book.

And

then I

drew . . .

a beautiful plane to fly us all there.

When we landed, we saw two giraffes,
a hippo and her baby, two lions, a rhino,
a monkey, a tiger, and a snake.

The elephant found a herd of friends
to play with.

Ettie and I gave them cookies.

But the poor aardvark was very
hot in the bright sun, so I drew . . .

a cool, dark burrow deep underground.

Ettie and I danced and sang with the elephant while the aardvark played the horn.

Then it was time to go home. But the elephant and the aardvark wanted to stay in Africa.

So we gave them big hugs and said good-bye.

Ettie wondered how we'd get home,
but I knew exactly what to do.

close the drawing book.

"That's what I call a happy ending!"
said Ettie as we left the zoo.
"Yes," I said. "I wonder what
we'll draw tomorrow."

Fancy Cards

The Burrow

Dear Danny and Ettie,
from deep down in my burrow
I send you spadefuls of love.
Aardvark

To Danny and Ettie
near the ZOO

Susak Cards

Dear Ettie and Danny,
I'm having a smashing time
with my new friends.
They all want red scarves.
Love, Elephant

To Ettie and Danny
c/o Somewhere

near the ZOO